WALT DISNEP's
Pinocchio

Pinocchio's
Nose
Grows

By Barbara Gaines Winkelman

Illustrated by Orlando de la Paz
and Paul Lopez

Random House 🏠 New York

Once there lived

a wood-carver.

The toy he loved most
was a puppet.
He called the puppet
Pinocchio.

One night,
a wishing star
twinkled in the sky.

The wood-carver
made a wish.
He wished that Pinocchio
were a real boy.

A blue light filled
the workshop.
The light turned into
the Blue Fairy!

She waved
her magic wand
over Pinocchio.

Pinocchio opened
his eyes!
"Am I a real boy?"
he asked.

"You may become
a real boy someday,"
said the Blue Fairy.

"But first, you must learn right from wrong," she said.

"How?" asked Pinocchio.

The Blue Fairy

asked Jiminy Cricket

to be Pinocchio's helper.

And then she left.

The wood-carver saw

Pinocchio.

He thought his wish

had come true.

He was very happy!

They danced and sang.

The wood-carver sent
Pinocchio off to school.

Pinocchio carried his book
and an apple for the teacher.

A cat and a fox
stopped Pinocchio.

"Come with us,"
the fox said.
"We will make you
a star!"

Jiminy Cricket called,
"Where are you going,
Pinocchio?"

Pinocchio did not listen.

He did not want to go

to school.

He wanted to be a star.

Pinocchio danced
on a stage.

He liked being a star!

But then he was
locked up in a cage.
"Help!" cried Pinocchio.
Jiminy Cricket could not
get Pinocchio out.

The Blue Fairy

heard his cries.

She came at once.

"Why are you not at school?" she asked. Pinocchio was afraid to tell the truth.

So he told a lie.

"Two monsters tied

me in a sack!"

His nose grew and grew!

"A lie is as plain
as the nose
on your face,"
said the Blue Fairy.

Pinocchio shook in fear.
"I guess lying is wrong,"
said Pinocchio.
He promised never
to lie again.

"Good," the Fairy said.
"You are learning."
She waved
her magic wand.

Pinocchio was free!

His nose was small again.

"Let's go home!"

said Jiminy Cricket.